THIS CANDLEWICK BOOK BELONGS TO:

painting

looking

counting

scowling

bouncing

bending

running

drinking

sitting

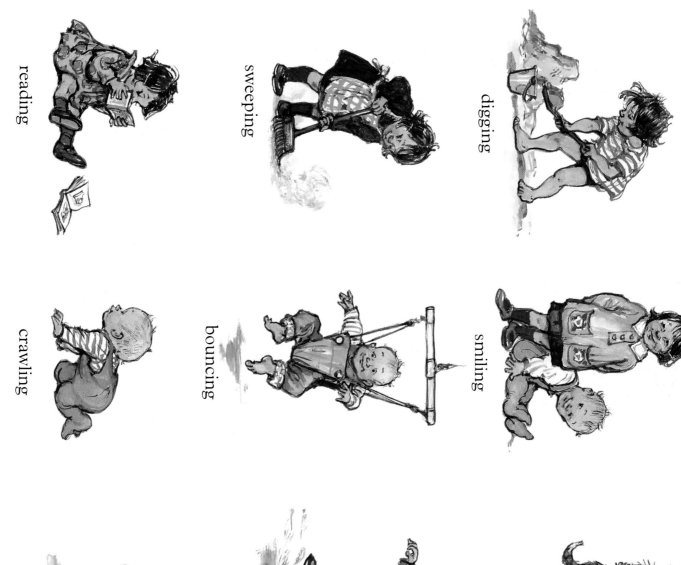

reading

sweeping

digging

crawling

bouncing

smiling

sucking

stamping

hugging

For Jack

Copyright © 1993 by Shirley Hughes

All rights reserved.

First U.S. paperback edition 1995

Library of Congress Cataloging-in-Publication Data

Hughes, Shirley.

Bouncing / Shirley Hughes.—1st U.S. ed.

Summary: A girl and her family enjoy many different kinds of bouncing.

ISBN 1-56402-128-9 (hardcover)—ISBN 1-56402-554-3 (paperback)

[1. Play—Fiction.] I. Title

PZ7.H87395Bo   1993   92-53001

[E]—dc20

2 4 6 8 10 9 7 5 3 1

Printed in Hong Kong

The pictures in this book were done in colored pencil,
watercolor, and pen line.

Candlewick Press
2067 Massachusetts Avenue
Cambridge, Massachusetts 02140

Bouncing

Shirley Hughes

CANDLEWICK PRESS
CAMBRIDGE, MASSACHUSETTS

When I throw my big shiny ball . . . .

it bounces away from me.

Then it rolls along the ground, and it stops.

Bounce, bounce, bounce, bounce, bounce!

I like bouncing too. In the mornings
I bounce on my bed,

and the baby bounces in his crib.

Mom and Dad's big bed is an even better place to bounce.

But Dad doesn't like being bounced
on in the early morning.

So we roll on the floor instead, and the
baby bounces on ME!

After breakfast he
does some dancing
in his baby bouncer,

and I do some dancing
to the radio.

At my play group there are big cushions on the floor where lots of children can bounce together.

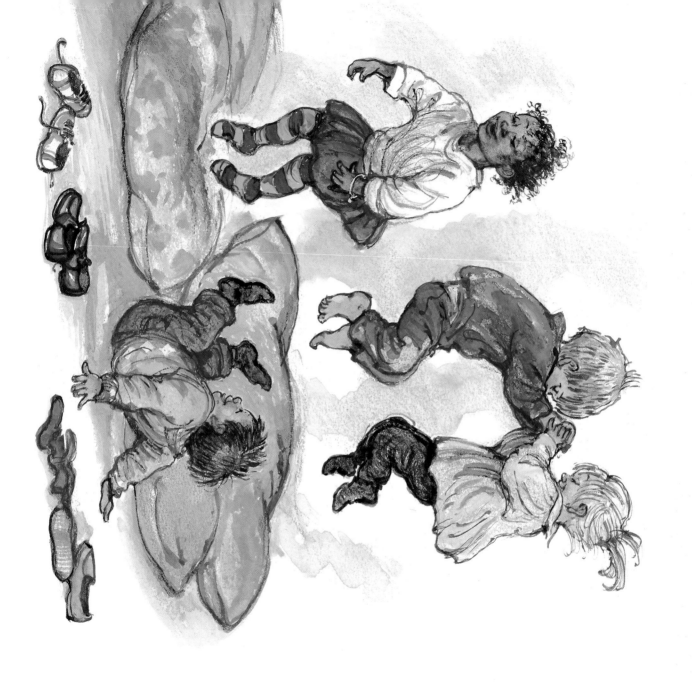

And at home there's a big sofa where we
can bounce when Mom isn't looking.

Grandpa and I know a good bouncing game.

I ride on his knees and we sing:

This is the way the ladies ride, trit-trot, trit-trot,

This is the way the gentlemen ride, giddy-up, giddy-up.

This is the way the farmers ride, clip-clop, clip-clop,

This is the way the jockeys ride, gallopy, gallopy,

and FALL OFF!

I like bouncing.

bounce, bounce,
bounce, bounce!

I bounce around all day . . .

Until in the end I stop bouncing,

and go to sleep.

looking

counting

scowling

painting

bouncing

bending

running

drinking

sitting

reading

sweeping

digging

crawling

bouncing

smiling

sucking

stamping

hugging

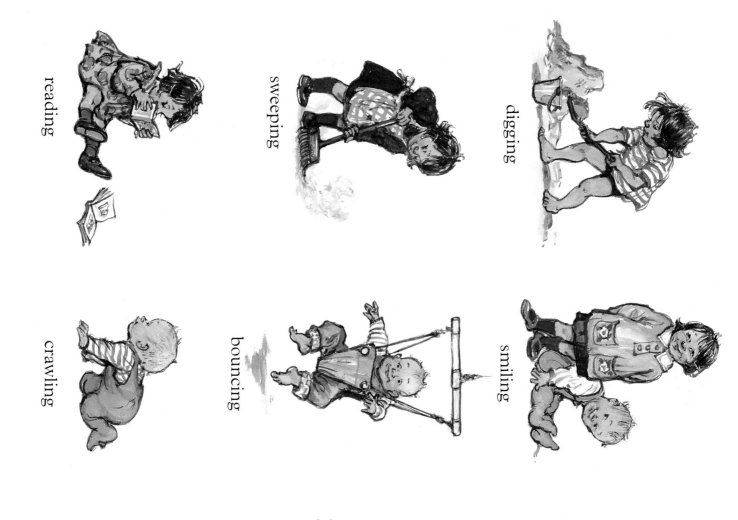

SHIRLEY HUGHES's affectionate drawings, unique warmth, and deep understanding of family life have given her a special place in the hearts of children and parents everywhere. Her many books, including *The Big Concrete Lorry* and *Out and About*, have received international acclaim. She says that "*Bouncing* is a very simple, accessible book intended for sheer enjoyment. But tucked inside is a small lesson about 'doing' words."

Also by Shirley Hughes:

Chatting
Giving
Hiding